A Banana in the Sun

Written by Jane Clarke
Illustrated by Camilla Galindo

Collins

Who's in this story?

Listen and say 🎧①

Peter

Jade

Teacher

Jack

Marty

Marty's class are painting pictures.

Marty's picture doesn't look like
a banana!

Marty paints a yellow picture.
His teacher asks, "What's in
your picture, Marty?"

Marty says, "It's a banana in the sun!"

Marty paints a brown picture.
Jade asks, "Is that a tree?"

Marty says, "It's a tree and a brown dog in mud!"

Marty paints a green picture.
He says, "It's a green frog on grass."

Jack says, "It's great!"

Marty paints a blue picture.
He says, "It's a blue bird in the sky."

Marty paints a red picture.

He says, "It's an apple swimming in tomato soup!"

Marty paints a carrot on an orange.

Marty paints black cats in a cave at night.

Peter says, "Nice picture!"

Marty's paper is white.

His teacher asks, "Is it clouds?"

Jade asks, "Is it rice?"

16

Jack asks, "Is it white bears in snow?"
Marty says, "No! It's paper to paint on!"

Marty's got paper. He's got lots of paints.

Marty loves colours.
What is Marty painting?

His teacher asks, "What is it, Marty?"

Marty says, "Can't you see? It's me!"

Picture dictionary

Listen and repeat

cave

cloud

grass

mud

sky

snow

soup

1 Look and order the story

2 Listen and say

Collins

Published by Collins
An imprint of HarperCollins*Publishers*
Westerhill Road
Bishopbriggs
Glasgow
G64 2QT

HarperCollins*Publishers*
1st Floor, Watermarque Building
Ringsend Road
Dublin 4
Ireland

William Collins' dream of knowledge for all began with the publication of his first book in 1819.

A self-educated mill worker, he not only enriched millions of lives, but also founded a flourishing publishing house. Today, staying true to this spirit, Collins books are packed with inspiration, innovation, and practical expertise. They place you at the center of a world of possibility and give you exactly what you need to explore it.

© HarperCollins*Publishers* Limited 2020

10 9 8 7 6 5 4 3 2

ISBN 978-0-00-839762-3

Collins® and COBUILD® are registered trademarks of HarperCollins*Publishers* Limited

www.collins.co.uk/elt

British Library Cataloguing in Publication Data

A catalogue record for this publication is available from the British Library.

Author: Jane Clarke
Illustrator: Camilla Galindo (Beehive)
Series editor: Rebecca Adlard
Commissioning editor: Fiona Undrill
Publishing manager: Lisa Todd
Product managers: Jennifer Hall and Caroline Green
In-house editor: Alma Puts Keren
Project manager: Emily Hooton
Editor: Emma Wilkinson
Proofreaders: Natalie Murray and Michael Lamb
Cover designer: Kevin Robbins
Typesetter: 2Hoots Publishing Services Ltd
Audio produced by id audio, London
Reading guide author: Emma Wilkinson
Production controller: Rachel Weaver
Printed and bound by: GPS Group, Slovenia

MIX
Paper from
responsible sources

FSC
www.fsc.org

FSC™ C007454

This book is produced from independently certified FSC™ paper to ensure responsible forest management.

For more information visit: **www.harpercollins.co.uk/green**

Download the audio for this book and a reading guide for parents and teachers at www.collins.co.uk/839762